Franklin's Secret Club

For Mira – P.B.

For Robin and his friends – B.C.

ISBN 0-590-13000-5

 Published by Scholastic Inc., 555 Broadway, New York, NY 10012, by arrangement with Kids Can Press Ltd.
Interior illustrations prepared with the assistance of Shelley Southern.

12 11 10 9 8 7 6 5 4 3 2 1 8 9/9 0 1 2 3/0

Printed in the U.S.A.

First Scholastic printing, September 1998

Franklin's Secret Club

Written by Paulette Bourgeois
Illustrated by Brenda Clark

SCHOLASTIC INC.
New York Toronto London Auckland Sydney

FRANKLIN could count by twos and tie his shoes. He liked to play on teams and join in games. Franklin belonged to the school choir and the arts and crafts club. He liked belonging and that's why Franklin decided to start his own club.

One day Franklin discovered a hideaway near his house. It was the perfect place for a club.

"We can have a secret password and a secret handshake," Franklin told Bear.

"And secret snacks?" asked Bear hopefully.

"With secret ingredients," Franklin laughed.

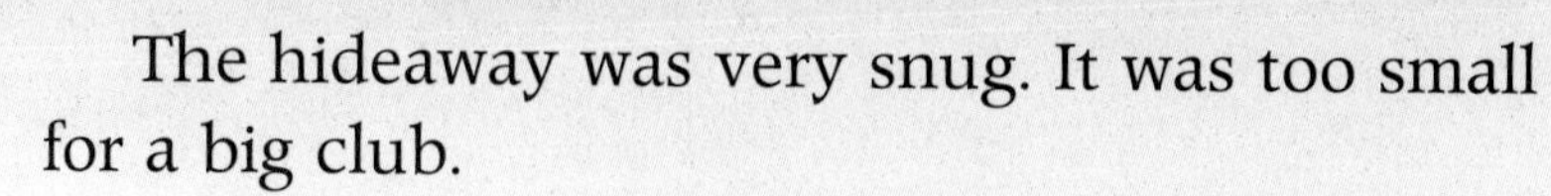

The hideaway was very snug. It was too small for a big club.

"I know," said Franklin. "Snail and Rabbit will fit. Let's ask them to join."

Together, Snail, Rabbit, Franklin, and Bear fixed up the clubhouse.

They called themselves the Secret Club.

The club members met every day after school. They ate blueberry muffins and made tin-can telephones. They made macaroni bracelets and gave them to one another.

Franklin was so busy doing secret things with the other club members that he almost forgot about the rest of his friends.

At school, everyone was being very nice to Franklin. Especially Beaver.

She saved Franklin a seat on the bus for three days in a row. She offered him the best part of her lunch. She even helped Franklin tidy up after art.

"Thank you, Beaver," said Franklin.

Beaver smiled. "Now can I join your club?"

Franklin was surprised. He didn't know that others wanted to join his club.

"Sorry, Beaver," said Franklin. "But we can't fit anyone else in the clubhouse."

"That's not a good reason," muttered Beaver. "And it's not fair. I'm going to start my own club."

"But ..." Franklin began, as Beaver left in a huff.

After school, Franklin's club had a treasure hunt.

Franklin didn't find a thing. He was upset because Beaver had been so angry.

"I told Beaver there just isn't room for more members," Franklin explained to Snail, Bear, and Rabbit.

They nodded sadly.

The next day Franklin and Bear did their secret handshake – two slaps and a tickle – and whispered the password, "Blueberries."

Bear flapped his arms, wiggled his fingers, wrinkled his nose, and said, "Fizzle-Fazzle, Diddle-Daddle, Ding-Dong-Bop!"

"What was that?" asked Franklin.

"The handshake and the password for Beaver's Adventure Club. Fox showed me."

"Oh," said Franklin.

The Secret Club members kept busy playing games.

Franklin had fun, but he'd heard that Beaver's club was even more fun.

"Today the adventurers are digging for dinosaurs," said Snail.

"The Adventure Club sure is amazing," sighed Bear.

"Sure is," said Franklin.

Franklin tried hard to think of secret things that were more exciting. The Secret Club members learned to write invisible letters with lemon juice, and one day they made a secret code.

But that very same day, the adventurers planned a trip to the moon.

Soon after, Franklin and his club members went to see Beaver's adventure headquarters.

There was a tree house to climb up to, a tire to swing from, a tent to play in, and a big sign that said, MEMBERS ONLY.

Franklin itched to join the Adventure Club.

"Now I know how Beaver felt," he said sadly. "Left out."

Suddenly, Franklin had an idea.

"Let's invite all the adventurers to join our club so *nobody* feels left out," he announced.

"But there's not enough room for everyone," said Bear.

"We can always meet outside," said Franklin. "Then there'll be plenty of room."

Beaver made a sign for their club headquarters. It said, "Secret Adventure Club."

Franklin made another sign. It said, "Everyone Welcome." He didn't want anybody to feel left out.